THE STINK BEFORE CHRISTMAS

For Meridon... who has no choice in whether she loves Christmas or not, because her daddy absolutely LOVES CHRISTMAS. Love you more though Meri... just x **SAM**

For Scarlett and Teddy, my babies who will grow up loving Christmas. Daddy loves you to the stars and back xx **MARK**

To Tabby, who made all my Christmases come at once **TOM**

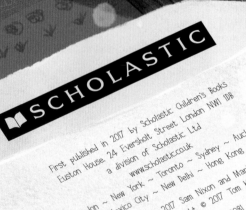

SCHOLASTIC

First published in 2017 by Scholastic Children's Books
Euston House, 24 Eversholt Street, London NW1 1DB
a division of Scholastic Ltd
www.scholastic.co.uk
London ~ New York ~ Toronto ~ Sydney ~ Auckland
Mexico City ~ New Delhi ~ Hong Kong

Text copyright © 2017 Sam Nixon and Mark Rhodes
Illustrations copyright © 2017 Tom Knight

PB ISBN 978 1407 18081 6

Written by
SAM and MARK

Illustrated by
TOM KNIGHT

THE STINK BEFORE CHRISTMAS

(with apologies to Clement Clarke Moore)

THE NORTH POLE

'Twas the night
before Christmas,
when all through the house
not a creature was stirring,
not even a **mouse...**

...But I'll tell you what was stirring: 'twas Santa's **big bottom!**

He was stuck on the toilet. He'd eaten something **rotten.**

THRRP!

SPLOT

He heard his dear wife shout.

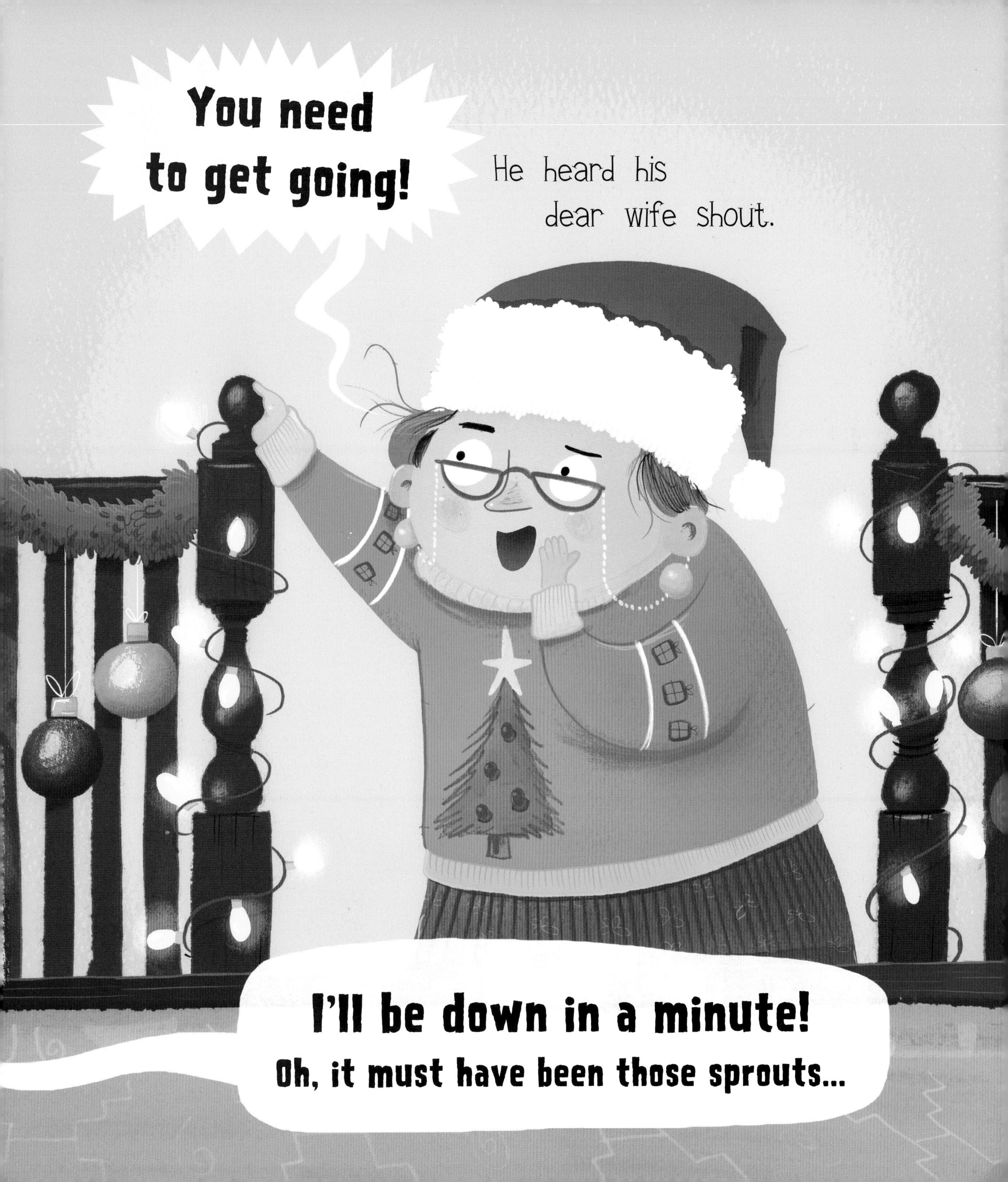

Finally Santa was dressed.
He was ready to go,

even though he felt like
his bum was going to **blow!**

I've packed you your favourite:
it's cabbage with baked beans.
Fly safe and remember,
try not to be seen!

And as he left
the North Pole,

he let out a little...

TRUMP!

Poor **Dasher**, and **Dancer**, and **Prancer**, and ... **Steve**
needed pegs on their noses
to survive Christmas Eve.

So on Santa flew, so fast and so high!

It should have been **awesome**,

but Santa wanted to **cry.**

His tummy felt sore.
'Twas all the **questionable** food!
Surely delivering the presents
would brighten the mood?

"**It's no use,**" Santa said,
"**But sadly it's true,**

**my bottom must burp,
– let's hope I don't poo!**"

He squeezed out a **pump.**
And his frown? It disappeared!

"Back to work," he said smiling,

...but something
felt **weird.**

Where were all
the presents?

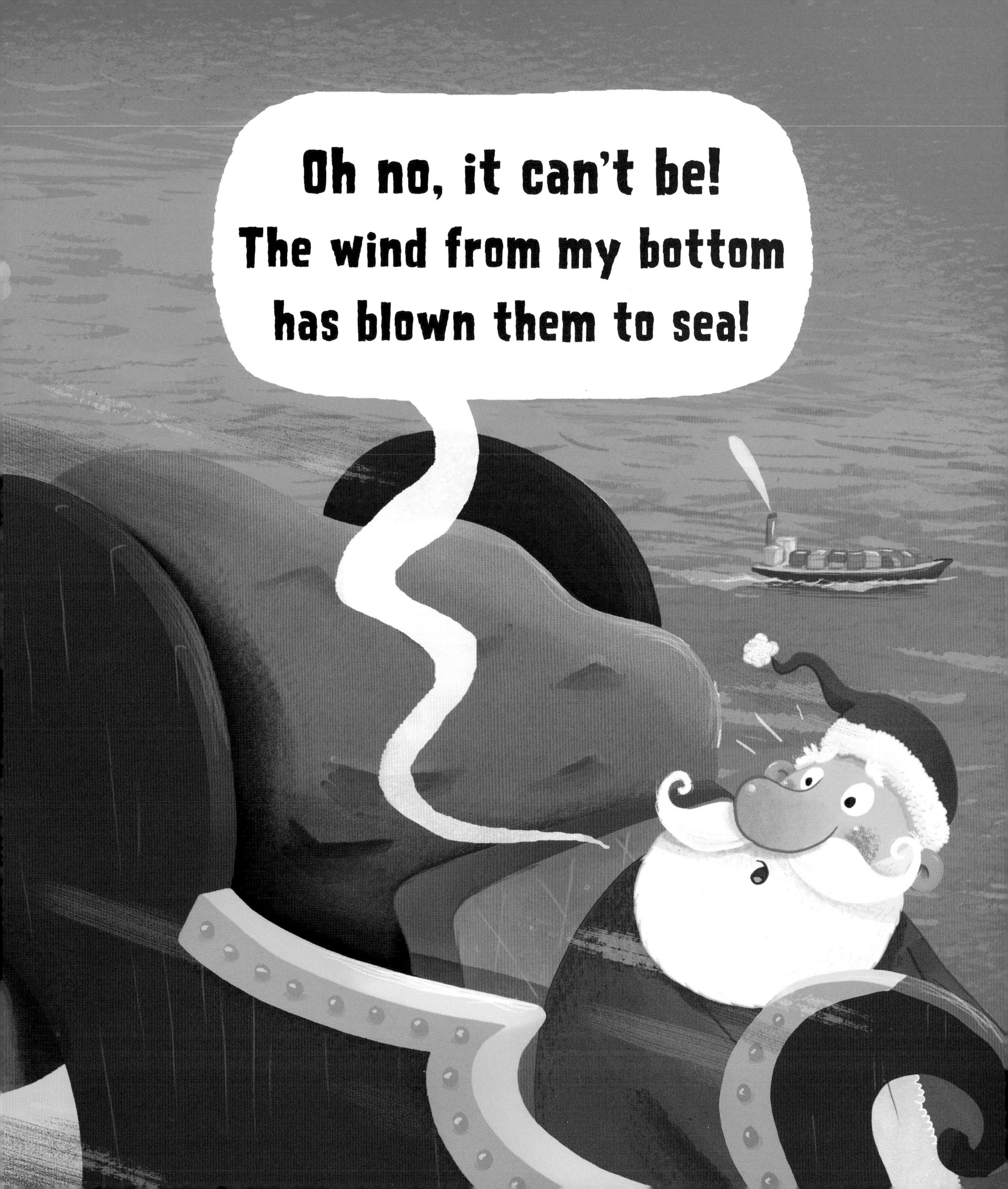
Oh no, it can't be!
The wind from my bottom
has blown them to sea!

So down Santa went...
Oh, **how fast** the reindeer flew!

"**We'll land on that rock.
That's what we'll do!**"

Santa pulled from his sack
his old fishing rod.

"We can't have these presents
all stinking of cod!"

As he **fished** the last parcel

onto his sleigh,

he noticed a **problem**

right there in the bay.

That **rock** he was perched on,
it made his face turn pale.

That's because it **wasn't**
a rock at all...

It was a **huge**...

HUMPBACK WHALE!!!!!!

"Oh, fly, reindeer, fly!"
Santa squealed in a panic,
"before this whale sinks us
just like the Titanic!"

But everyone **knows**
reindeer can't launch from water!
And Santa still had gifts for
every son and daughter.

He needed a gust of wind,
—a boost by some means!

Then he noticed the reindeer
scoffing his **cabbage**
with **baked beans.**

**Now's no time for eating –
This whale's got the huff!**

And just as he said that,
Prancer let out a **MASSIVE...**

...GUFF!!!

The guff was **so big**
it flew them all around the world.
That guff was **SO** big

they delivered to **every** boy and girl!

Santa **enjoyed**
that Christmas Eve,
even though he **was**
in a bit of a grump.
"Merry Christmas to all,"
he exclaimed,

"and to all a good..."

TRUMP!